"Millions of spiritual creatures walk the earth
Unseen, both when we wake, and when we sleep."

—John Milton, PARADISE LOST

EVIDENCE
of
Angels

SUZA SCALORA

WITH

Francesca Lia Block

HARPER

An Imprint of HarperCollinsPublishers

DO ANGELS EXIST? Or are we alone?

What happens after we die and leave this earth?

These were the questions that plagued me after the death of my beloved, Gustav. I have had faith but not always, and not recently. After Gustav passed on, a darkness descended upon me I feared would never leave. I had once photographed fairies, witches and wizards: Now these magical creatures would not appear to me no matter how hard I looked for them.

It was as if my vision into the unseen world had disappeared. All I saw was a city wounded by destruction.

I wandered out into the city every day, holding my camera but ready to drop it onto the pavement or into a trash bin. My heart felt not unlike a broken camera itself: Something that had once been able to capture the essence of life was now only a box of metal and glass.

One day I could hardly rise from my bed. Rain poured down outside and I found myself wishing I would never have to go out into the world again. But late in the afternoon the rain stopped and a beam of sunlight came through the window, illuminating a picture I had taken of Gustav. As I stared into his eyes, I heard a distinct, though faint, voice. It whispered, "Stand up. Everything in your life has meaning. Your journey is to find it." The voice resonated in my heart. I got up, dressed, grabbed my camera and went outside.

Now I was ready.

The first place I knew I must visit was the city library, whose chambers I had haunted while researching my various projects. I had not been there since Gustav's death. The cool marble rooms were filled with mahogany tables, gold leaf columns and alabaster statues of heroes from days past. I sat, my mind spinning and body suddenly weary again.

At that moment I noticed a tall man with golden hair and an uncanny light coming off his body. The light was so intense around his face that I could not make out his features. He approached me and said, "Your eyes only see what your mind understands. Open your heart to the miracles that surround you every day." Now when I try to recall him speaking I cannot remember his mouth moving or the actual sound of the words, but I know I heard them.

The man handed me a large book with a tattered leather cover and gold leaf edging the pages entitled *Divine Light: Angels*. Before I could say anything, he was gone, without a sound, though the marble floors made even the lightest of footsteps echo.

I opened the book and began to read.

DIVINE LIGHT: ANGELS

In ancient times, all humans were in alignment with the Angelic Realm because the collective unconscious believed in their existence. Currently, the interest in angels and fairies is generally regarded as the "stuff of childhood dreams." Eventually, all humans will regain their sight into the Unseen World and communication and connection with the angels and other nonphysical guides will return.

After reading this passage, my sense of hope was renewed. The next day I ventured out into the streets. I snapped photo after photo of various parts of the city, making sure not to look at what my camera had recorded until I was alone. When I returned home to my studio, I lit some candles, took a deep breath and studied the images.

ALTHOUGH MY CITY looked vibrant to me again, I was disappointed not to find anything unusual, until I came to the last photograph. It was nothing like the rest: abstractions of color and light filled the page. I went back to my book and found an enlightening entry.

Beings from the "Unseen World" can choose to appear in any form, depending on the perception of the viewer. Angels are from the nonphysical realm, an amorphous world constructed of energy, difficult to see with the human eye. The archetypal image of the angel as a human with wings is what most of us imagine. At times it is easier to perceive an ethereal aberration of light and color. But ways of seeing strengthen as the journey continues and belief grows.

Angel of Grief

The next day I woke refreshed and enlivened. After I dressed and ate, I stepped out into the day. It was clear after the rain, and the city glowed with a strange, ethereal light as I wandered about. Later that afternoon I found myself at the cemetery. The light I had noticed was even more mysterious here, as if it emanated from the tombstones themselves. Discreetly I took out my camera and began taking pictures. Here are the words I heard when I printed the photo of my first clearly visible angel.

"When you are grief stricken, call upon me for guidance. Falling into the depths of grief is closing off your heart. It is the loss of hope. When you step into the darkness, you become the darkness. There is a cycle of life that moves throughout your world: birth and death. Awaken to your feelings of faith and courage. You have the strength to go on."

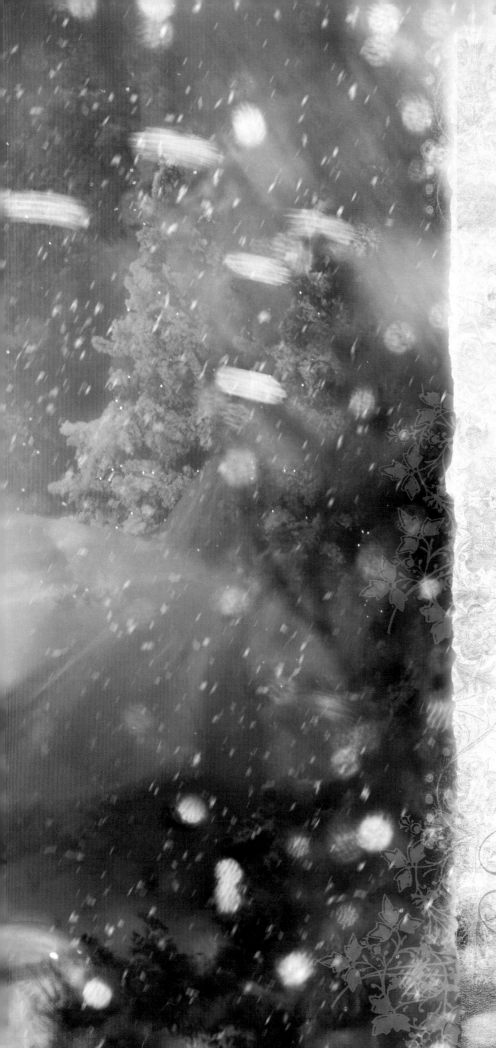

Angel of Winter

After this encounter, the angels came to me on an almost daily basis. As autumn turned to winter, I had no impulse to stay inside and hide but braved the weather with my heavy wool coat, galoshes and ever-ready camera. Though my fingers were almost too numb with cold to take the photographs, I persevered, driven by the joy I would experience when I printed out my work each night in my warm studio and by the voices that accompanied the images.

"The storm is fierce and black, yet a ray of light shines through the shadows toward a new day, toward hope."

Angel of Courage

The street was empty after a snowstorm. I stepped onto the sidewalk and was blinded by the bright sunlight. When I raised my hand to shield my eyes, a vision unfolded before me. The power of it and the words I heard made me forget the gnawing chill that had reached into my bones. All I knew was warmth.

"There will be many times during your journey that you will want to give up. It is the force of your will that pushes you to make the choice to go on, to take the next step. True courage is the strength to face your inner fears and self-doubt. Within you is the courage to carry on, even when you think your strength is gone. Remember you are not alone, and there is always help."

Angel of Healing

I no longer had any doubts as to the existence of angels. All of a sudden I had a desire to connect with others who had had similar experiences, so I began hanging my photographs around the city—on walls and lampposts and fences. I included my email address, angels@myth.com, and my P.O. box. Three days later my first letter arrived.

It has come to our awareness that illness in the body is not to be feared but seen as a guide, reminding us to live our lives in alignment with our soul's purpose. How, we may wonder, do we accomplish such a task? This is the purpose of the Angel of Healing who waits at the bedside of every patient; all we need do is ask. If we are unable to raise our voices in this direction, due to lack of faith or a similarly ill spirit, we may turn to others who may take it upon themselves to write a letter for us. This estimable service will activate that waiting being, bring profound solace to the patient as well as ourselves and ultimately deliver us all closer to our ideal: a civilization that can transcend suffering and torment as we now know it.

Dear Suza,

I am writing to you on behalf of my younger sister, Lisa. She became sick over a year ago. We spent months visiting doctor after doctor, but no one could diagnose her illness. Her suffering is apparent, although she tries to present a brave demeanor. She doesn't believe in angels, and I have had my crises of faith many times in my life, but deep in my heart I know angels are there waiting for us to call on them. After seeing your pictures I ask that you visit us and see if you can photograph the unseen presence I believe is here so that Lisa may believe it too and heal.

With gratitude,
Sarah Newton

Sarah's letter moved me deeply but also frightened me. What if I could not help her? I consulted my book on the topic of the Angel of Healing. Once again, the book held the answer I sought. I only had to open its cover.

I went to visit Sarah and took this photograph.

Angel of Trust

As time passed, I continued to roam the city each day. I thought of Gustav at every turn, remembering the things we had done, the sound of his voice, the way his face looked in different light. I frequented the park where we ran races, fed the swans and had picnics. Instead of causing me pain, the memories inspired me to take more and more pictures. Somehow it made me feel closer to him. Here are some of the angels I encountered, along with the words that I heard accompanying them.

"There is an invisible curtain that separates the physical world from the nonphysical world. We create the curtain with our disbelief and cynicism. Break through your disbelief. Trust that everything in your life has meaning."

Angel of
Compassion

"These are the gifts we wish to share
with you: compassion, charity and
hope. Recognize and accept your
own humanity and you will embrace
the humanity of others."

Angel of Love

"Love is itself an angel waiting to manifest.
When it does so, it can challenge and overcome
all anguish. This is the time to call me forth
from the darkness, selflessly, purely and without
attachment to the outcome. Every endeavor,
action and word will be blessed by the angels
when your intention is Love."

Angel of Knowledge

"All true knowledge
resides within you."

Angel of Spring

"Spring, with its cascading blossoms lit from within as
if by divinity, is the season of renewal and rebirth ...
nothing truly dies. Your soul is eternal."

"We are with you."

Angel of
Sorrow

"Fear is an absence of light, a darkness that seeps into your

soul. It prevents you from being all that you are,

a beacon of light for all to see."

"I appear differently to everyone who sees me, but I reside in every heart the same. No matter how much chaos rages around you, I can be found within if you close your eyes and follow the rise and fall of your breath. My face will appear to you in a form you are able to recognize."

Angel of Peace

Angel of Children's Dreams

Each day more letters arrived, detailing experiences with angels. One was from a six-year-old boy, written in an adult's hand but signed by him and illustrated with a large drawing of a winged creature rendered in violet crayon.

Dillon's mention of the violet figure, as well as my observation of the angels I had photographed, made me wonder if there was a connection between color and these divine beings.

Dear Suza,

I had really, really bad dreams. A monster was hiding in my closet and another one was waiting under my bed. I tried to be brave and pretend they weren't there, but I could hear them moving around.

I told my grandma, and she said there was one sure way to get rid of the monsters. I should call to the Angel of Children's Dreams and ask her to help me have good dreams. That night I asked the angel to make the monsters go away. I had funny dreams and no monsters. I even saw her standing outside the window a couple of times. She was a pretty light purple color. Maybe you could come take her picture sometime.

From your friend,

DILLON CONNER

THE FOLLOWING TEXT in the book confirmed this idea: Throughout the ages, color has been associated with visions of angels. The glowing angels are often referred to as the "Illuminated Beings." Their enormous power of love flows to create abstractions of light in a vast array of colors. An angelic encounter may reveal many colors. Ancient writings have alluded to a "Divine Light" carried down by the angels from the heavens as a gift for humankind.

GREEN:
renewal, abundance, health

BLUE:
calm, tranquility, clarity

GOLD:
illumination, awareness, spirituality

PINK:
love, patience, friendship

ORANGE:
motivation, courage, creativity

YELLOW:
intelligence, hope, inspiration

RED:
passion, energy, ambition

PURPLE:
mysticism, wisdom, magic

Angel of Gratitude

Dear Ms. Scalora,

My mother always said I had a guardian angel watching over me. Through the years I'd forgotten about the stories she told me when I was young. I was reminded late one spring night while driving back from my mom's house. I had my five-month-old daughter, Madeline, in the backseat. Out of nowhere a huge piece of metal appeared; I hit it and lost control of the car. We spun into the oncoming lane of traffic. As soon as the car stopped moving, I tried the door but it wouldn't budge. I panicked. All I could do was pray. Then I felt something brush my cheek and say, "Take your child and open the door." Amazingly, Madeline was still sleeping; I picked her up and tried the door again. It opened without effort. The traffic had stopped and I was able to make it to the side of the road. A moment later the car ignited.

A man ran up to me and asked where the other woman was who had been in the car with us. I told him there was no one else. He said he was sure he'd seen a woman in white sitting there.

I know that was my guardian angel my mother always spoke of. I'm sure Madeline has one too. Sometimes I find her laughing and cooing at something or someone I can't see.

Many blessings,
Barbara Rosemont

Dear Suza,

My fiancé had just broken off our engagement two weeks before our wedding. I'd been crying all night. I got up early to take a walk in the park to clear my head. The morning sun was beginning to peek over the trees when suddenly it felt like the rays of light were touching the top of my head. I was immersed in warmth and well-being. I was sure an angel had touched me. The sadness I'd felt was gone, replaced by a joyfulness I hadn't felt for many years. As I sat basking in the presence of the angel, I was reminded of the doubt I'd felt during my engagement: a small voice inside me had said my fiancé was not the one for me. But every time those feelings arose, I did my best to ignore them. I can see clearly now he did what I could not do. This was a gift and the angels helped me see it that way.

Sincerely,
Crystal

MOVED BY CRYSTAL'S LETTER, I went out
with my camera again. That day, everything around me appeared
to be vibrating with energy. I walked across the street to sit in the
park. A soft breeze rustled through the trees, making the leaves
appear to glitter. In a barely audible whisper I heard the words . . .

"We are here to help . . . you are never
given more than you can manage."

Angel of Clarity

"Open your heart, live in each moment.

Only then will you see clearly."

loneliness

loss   fear

As I moved through my journey, reborn to the unseen world,

visited by angels, I awakened to my life's purpose: I had been given

the gift to see angels, and to share this with others.

                                                          love

acceptance

            trust

Angel of Charity

"Each time we give to others we are closer to what is truly divine."

EVERY DAY MORE ANGELS APPEARED.

I was beginning to see not only the manifestations of emotion that took the form of angels, but I also saw the angels themselves as the usually invisible threads of energy that bind us all together. I had seen angels in the library, in the park, at the fountain, almost everywhere I turned in the city, and at all the places I had shared with Gustav. I felt I could see the essence of everything–the trees, the flowers and the people on the streets. The city had never looked so beautiful or so alive to me. I had shared my vision of the angels with others. I rarely felt alone anymore, and my despair at the loss of Gustav had faded. It was only at bedtime that I was afraid my grief would return, that I would dream of Gustav without my guides to protect me and remind me that I was still loved and safe.

But I began to realize that this went against everything the angels had taught me. So one night, I decided to ask for guidance in my dreams.

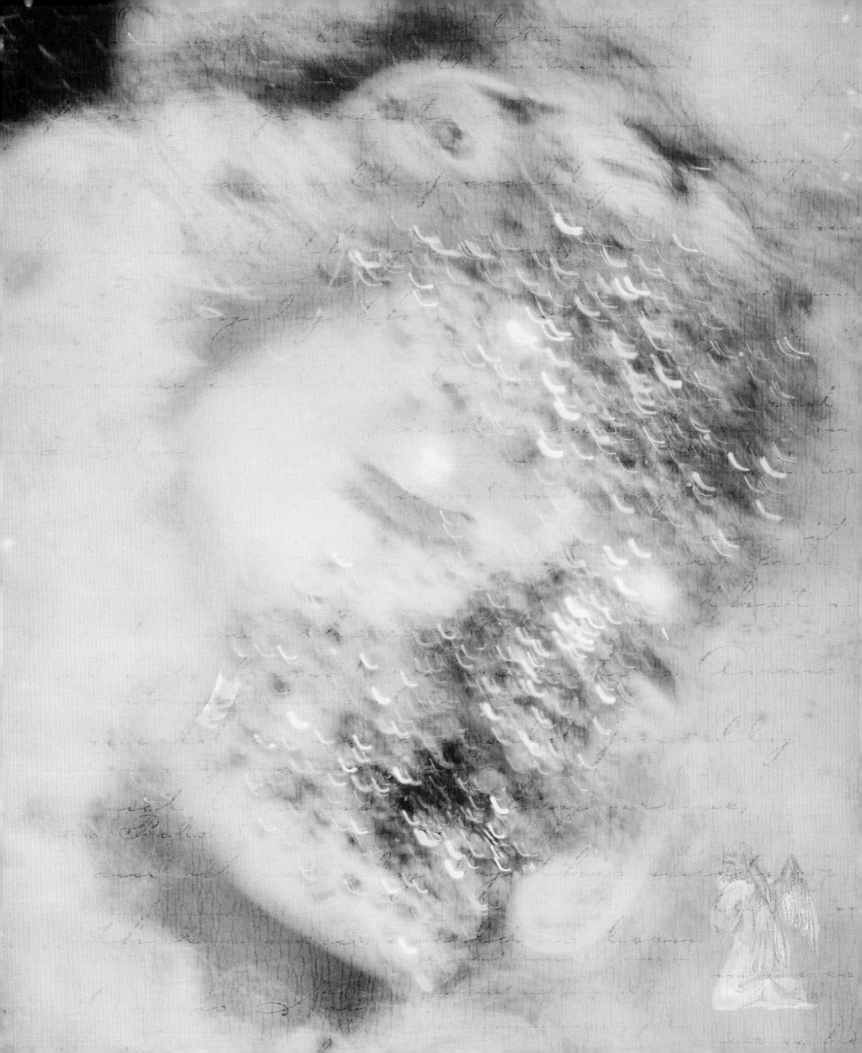

Angel of Wisdom

A large angel appeared before me. The light was dazzling. It felt as if I were spinning down a long tunnel, stunning colors engulfing me. When I woke in the morning there was a new photo, one I had not remembered taking. Once again, as I looked at the picture, I heard words as if a voice were whispering in my ear.

"Not long ago you lost your connection to the unseen world. There is so much more to life than what your eyes can see and what your mind understands. We are always sending you signs; will you open your heart to our messages?"

IT HAS BEEN ALMOST A YEAR since I lost Gustav.

Last night I had my first dream about him since his death. In my dream he put his face against mine and I felt the words enter my heart, though he did not speak a single one aloud.

"Can't you feel me with you? I'm still here, closer than you can imagine. Even though you can't see me . . . the love you thought you lost will never disappear. It is within you, always and forever. You are love."

I awoke to a sense of peace I'd never experienced before. With such clarity I could see the perfection of my life—the beauty, the grace and blessings given to me. I am in awe of the magnificence.

My prayer is that this book will support you in your journey. Love is eternal: This is my living proof.

Suza Scalora

This book is dedicated
to every person who has ever
felt alone.

ACKNOWLEDGMENTS

Throughout this journey, many, many kindhearted souls have supported me both with this book and in my life.

I am eternally grateful to my husband, David Lee Jones, for all his love and support. You will always be my prince among men.

Joanna Cotler for being the first one to see the potential of this book: Her vision and belief are invaluable gifts.

Francesca Lia Block for her brilliance, generosity and words.

My agent, Lydia Wills at Paradigm, you are an angel.

Antonia Markiet, I am blessed to have the gift of your infinite wisdom and precious guidance.

Heidi Henneman for her dedication and enthusiasm in producing this book.

I am exceedingly grateful for the generosity of the following people and organizations: Glenn Vanderlinden at CSC for ARRI Lighting; Hasselblad Cameras; MAC Cosmetics; Ken Madsen at Graphic Systems Group; Martin Izquierdo Studios; DJ, James and Juan at Vision On; Lis Pearson at the New York Public Library; Errol at American Foliage; and Sarah at Oliphant Studios.

I received enormous support and help from the following people, for which I am extremely grateful: Alma Melendez, Jennifer Kilberg, Chris Keohane aka Salty, Ralph Siciliano, Susan McCarthy, Robin Schoen, Wesley O'Meara, Mako, Vassilis Kokkinidis, Martin Christopher, Miok, Alberto Guzman, Alejandra Nerizagal, Paul Innis, Emma Prichard, Michele Garziano, Janeiro Gonzalez, Grayson Craddock, Clare Chong, Liz McClean, Charles Schindler, Lois Turner, Kara Delle Donne, Lynnea Scalora, Vanessa Varela, Neda Abghari, Anne, Elena, Marlene, Nadia, Cynthia, Angel, Aiji, Hudson Dinh, Emma, Lucia, Graciela, Rachael, Wendi, Nicole, Tori, Nancy, Omar, Gia, Rick, Jessica, Mikali, Leif and Christina, Nolin, Lucia, Timmy and Jacob.

I am particularly grateful to the amazing team at HarperCollins; it is a joy to work with all of you: Karen Nagel, Alyson Day, Ruiko Tokunaga, Matt Adamec and Sarah Hoy.

A special thanks to Gary Zukav, Linda Francis and the ESP participants for their spiritual partnership, inspiration and guidance.

And finally, thank you to all my angels and teachers, both physical and nonphysical, who always support me in choosing to see the love and joy that surround me every day.